AF575451

CAR TECHNOLOGY

BY JAMES BOW

childsworld.com

Published by The Child's World®
800-599-READ • www.childsworld.com

Photography Credits

Photographs ©: STRF/Star Max/IPx/AP Images, cover, 1; Shutterstock Images, 5, 13, 18, 21, 26; iStockphoto, 6, 17; Étienne Lenoir/Le Monde Illustré, 8; Russell Lee/Library of Congress, 10; National Photo Company Collection/Library of Congress, 14; Spencer Grant/Science Source, 22, 25 (top); Felix Mizioznikov/Shutterstock Images, 25 (middle); Mike Mareen/Shutterstock Images, 25 (bottom); Flystock/Shutterstock Images, 28

ISBN Information
9781503869813 (Reinforced Library Binding)
9781503881280 (Portable Document Format)
9781503882591 (Online Multi-user eBook)
9781503883901 (Electronic Publication)

LCCN 2022951195

Printed in the United States of America

ABOUT THE AUTHOR

James Bow is the author of five novels and more than 75 juvenile nonfiction books. He enjoys cars and trains. He loves cities, like his hometown of Toronto, Canada, where people can easily walk where they need to go.

CONTENTS

FAST FACTS

- In the early 1800s, steam engines were used to power machines. But they were large and hard to use. Internal **combustion** engines were smaller and more **efficient**. They made modern cars possible.
- People originally had to crank car engines by hand to start them. This sometimes resulted in injuries. Electric starters made the process safer.
- The three-point seat belt design reduced injuries from car crashes.
- The anti-lock braking system (ABS) helps keep cars from sliding on slippery roads. The system quickly pumps the brakes so the tires don't lock up.
- Electric cars run on battery power. They are better for the environment than cars that run on gas and diesel fuel.
- Self-driving cars may someday reduce the number of deaths from car accidents. These cars help remove human error from driving.

As car technology has advanced, cars have become safer for drivers and passengers. ►

CHAPTER ONE

THE INTERNAL COMBUSTION ENGINE

One September morning in 1863, a man named Étienne Lenoir climbed into a new kind of vehicle. It looked like a wooden cart with three wheels. It was called the Hippomobile. One small wheel was right underneath the driver, who sat on a long bench. There were two larger wheels on each side near the back. **Pistons** and gears would turn the wheels. If the engine in Lenoir's Hippomobile worked, it would change the world.

Lenoir started the engine. Sparks flew from the **ignition** system. The wheels began to turn. The Hippomobile was moving! Lenoir could hear a rhythm of small explosions coming from the engine. His machine turned the energy from those blasts into motion. Gas from burning coal fueled the engine.

◀ **Étienne Lenoir was born in Belgium. He eventually moved to France, where he invented his internal combustion engine.**

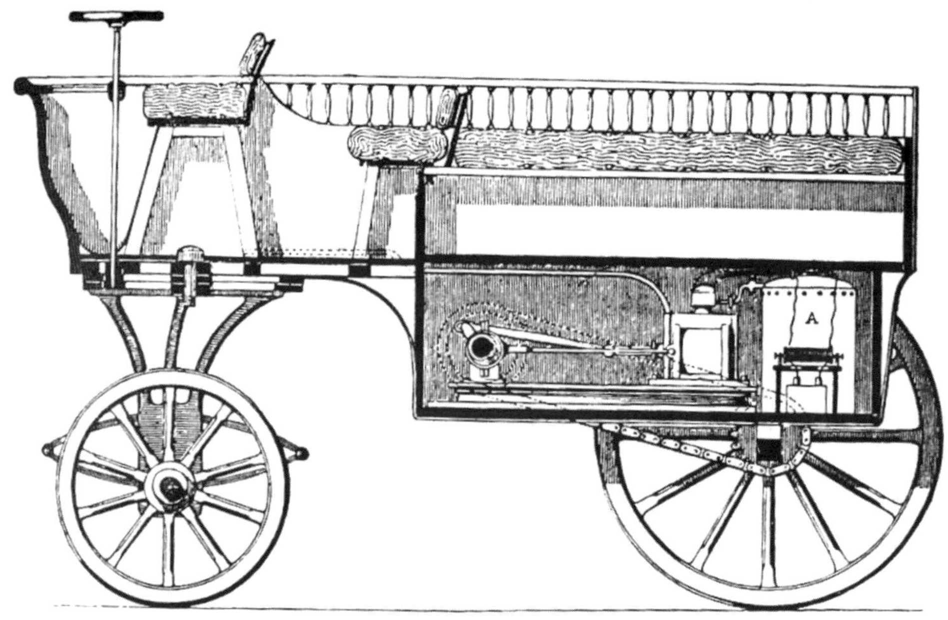

▲ **Behind the Hippomobile's driver, there were bench seats for up to seven passengers.**

Engines in modern gas-powered cars work the same way. But Lenoir's Hippomobile was not as powerful as today's cars.

That morning, Lenoir drove his Hippomobile through Paris, France, where he worked. His Hippomobile was probably not much faster than someone walking. Lenoir had to stop many times. His engine needed a lot of fuel. The Hippomobile was not very practical. But Lenoir's engine worked. It was the first trip of its kind. Lenoir's Hippomobile was an early working example of his internal combustion engine.

Before Lenoir's invention, most engines used steam to create motion. Steam engines burn coal or wood to boil water. The water turns to steam and the steam expands.

It pushes against the sides of its container. The pressure of this steam can turn a wheel. This motion can then be used to run machines or vehicles.

However, steam engines needed large boilers. It took a long time to heat the water. People had to keep shoveling fuel into the fire to keep it burning. Lenoir's motor was more efficient. It could move smaller things, such as carts or pumps. This meant it could be used in more places than steam engines.

Since then, other inventors have made improvements to Lenoir's engine. Scottish inventor Dugald Clerk added a second cylinder and piston. The movement from one piston started the explosion for the second. This movement then triggered the original piston again. Clerk's improvement created a continuous cycle of movement. Lenoir's partner, Alfonse Beau de Rochas, came up with the idea for a four-cylinder engine. His changes made engines faster and more reliable.

Lenoir is remembered as a great inventor. But he did not get rich from his internal combustion engine. He sold his engine **patent** early and began inventing more things. Other inventors would later improve on his engine designs. Lenoir couldn't imagine the impact his inventions would have in the future. But one day, more than one billion cars worldwide would use engines like his.

KLAHOMA
53T177

CHAPTER TWO

THE ELECTRIC STARTER AND CAR KEYS

James stared at the front of his car in dread. He tried to mentally prepare himself for the dangerous process of starting his car. Trips to the countryside with his girlfriend shouldn't start this way, he thought.

It was 1899. Cars had been around for a few decades. Most were powered by internal combustion engines. They had gotten bigger and faster, but the process of starting them had not changed much. Someone still needed to turn the engine. This moved the pistons to start the first few explosions before the engine could turn on its own. As car engines got more powerful, this process became harder and more dangerous.

James took a deep breath and turned the hand crank. The engine let out a bang, but then it stalled. He turned the crank faster. The engine sputtered. Suddenly there was a loud *bang*!

◄ **Although most cars used electric starters by the 1920s, some cars were still made with hand cranks for many years to come.**

The hand crank spun and whacked James's hands. The car jerked forward, knocking him to the ground.

James scrambled to his feet. He looked across the hood and saw his girlfriend's frantic look. She was gripping the steering wheel and the handbrake. There must be a better way, James thought. If only the engine could start itself.

An inventor in New York had been having the same thought. Clyde Coleman wanted to find a better way to start cars. He designed a small electric motor to do this. The **torque** from the electric motor could briefly crank the engine and start the car.

Coleman got a patent for his idea in 1903, but he sold the patent to the Delco Company to build his electric motor. However, the idea was too difficult and expensive at first. When Delco was bought out by General Motors, Coleman's idea landed on the desk of engineer Charles Kettering.

Kettering saw that the invention needed adjustments, but it was a good start. A **prototype** electric self-starter was added to a Cadillac in 1911. It became standard in Cadillac models the next year. Other carmakers used similar designs. By 1920, nearly every car being made had a self-starter. This meant people could start their cars with the push of a button.

Keys had been used to lock car doors since 1910. In 1949, the car company Chrysler created a key that started the engine, too.

▲ **Historic cars from the 1910s can be seen in museums around the world.**

Now, a driver had a single key that would unlock the car's doors and start its engine. Electric starters had made cars safer and more reliable, and keys made the process even easier. These features have become standard in modern cars.

DC

CHAPTER THREE

SEAT BELTS

Nils Bohlin stood in his laboratory. It was 1958, and he was thinking about people who had been seriously injured in car accidents. Bohlin was not a doctor. He was the chief safety engineer at Volvo Car Corporation. He knew that car crashes could cause injuries to passengers' spines and organs. Even if they were wearing seat belts, something could still go wrong.

Seat belts were invented in the late 1800s to help keep pilots safe inside gliders. Edward J. Claghorn patented a seat belt design in February 1885 to protect taxi riders in New York City. Many cars did not have seat belts until much later. In 1920, the most popular car had a top speed of about 45 miles per hour (72 kmh). At those speeds, people did not see a need for seat belts.

◄ Even though cars were slower in the 1920s than they are today, car accidents were still dangerous—especially without modern seat belts.

But as cars got faster in the 1930s, car accidents got worse. Many people died. Doctors found that seat belts kept passengers in their seats. The seat belts saved lives. Doctors showed their studies to car companies and the US government. Car companies started adding seat belts to their cars.

When Bohlin began working at Volvo, the seat belts in the company's cars were very different than they are today. At the time, a seat belt was a single belt strapped across the waist. Bohlin saw problems with this design. The seat belt kept people inside the car during a crash, but their upper bodies were yanked forward. This could cause severe injuries.

Bohlin saw ways to fix the design of seat belts. The strap shouldn't just hold someone's lower body in the seat. The seat belt needed to secure a passenger's upper body, too. But he also knew that seat belts needed to be simple to put on. Bohlin wanted to design a seat belt that could be buckled with only one hand. His solution was a belt that goes across a passenger's chest and then across the lap. The seat belt was buckled low against the hip. This was a three-point seat belt. It kept a person's upper body secure.

It was a simple and effective design. Bohlin and Volvo were happy to share it with other car companies. In 1966, the United States required all US vehicles to have seat belts.

▲ **Cars today still use the three-point seat belt that Bohlin designed.**

In 1970, the state of Victoria in Australia passed a law that drivers and passengers had to wear seat belts. Other countries followed this with their own laws. Governments launched safety campaigns that encouraged drivers and passengers to buckle up. There have been many other car safety advances over the years. But seat belts like the ones Bohlin invented are still used today.

IMO-181

CHAPTER FOUR

ANTI-LOCK BRAKES

Rachel was driving down a winding mountain road. She was going fast and took a sharp turn. The wet roadway shone under the glare of her headlights.

Rachel rounded another curve and spotted a deer. She slammed on the brakes. The car screeched. But something was wrong. Her car was still moving, and the steering wheel would not turn. Her car was heading for the edge of the road.

She realized she had slammed her brakes so hard that the wheels locked. They were sliding with the rest of the car. Fighting her instinct, Rachel took her foot off the brake pedal. Now she could steer again. However, the deer was still ahead of her. Over and over, she pressed the brake pedal down and then released it. This is called pumping the brakes.

◄ **Anti-lock brakes are still effective on slippery roads. Before ABS, driving in poor weather conditions was more dangerous.**

By doing this, Rachel slowed down her car without locking the wheels. She came to a stop a few feet from the deer.

The problem with locking brakes was clear to many inventors in the 1900s. In 1928, German engineer Karl Wessel designed a system that prevented wheels from locking. But Wessel's system was just an idea. It would be too difficult and expensive to put into vehicles.

Later, Mario Palazzetti had an idea. He was an engineer for the Italian carmaker Fiat. He designed a car system that could detect when the wheels locked. His anti-lock braking system (ABS) could pump the brakes faster than a driver could. ABS can pump the brakes as fast as twenty times per second. In 1978, Mercedes-Benz introduced a newer model of ABS. In the 1990s, ABS became standard for all Mercedes-Benz cars. Other car manufacturers quickly followed. This system makes sure that drivers can control how they stop. It has prevented countless crashes and saved many lives.

Rachel knew how to get back control of her car. By pumping the brakes, she was able to slow the car down and still be able to steer. But now, drivers don't have to worry about their brakes locking. The anti-lock braking systems in their cars pump the brakes for them.

**In many cars, a light on the dashboard ►
illuminates when ABS is active.**

ANTILOCK
BRAKE
UNLEADED
FUEL ONLY
F

ELECTRIC VEHICLE
CHARGER

CHAPTER FIVE

ELECTRIC CARS

It was 1997. Jackson punched in the five-digit ignition code to his new Electric Vehicle 1 (EV1). It felt weird to start a car without a key. He slowly pulled out of the dealership's parking lot in the first mass-produced electric car. The car was made by General Motors. It was sleek and red. It looked like something from the future.

Jackson wanted to test out the car's speed. A quick glance at the dashboard told Jackson the car's battery was full. He was ready to drive. He zoomed from 0 to 60 miles per hour (96.5 kmh) in 8.9 seconds. He could not wait to show his friends.

Unfortunately, the EV1 had some drawbacks. The battery life was used up quickly, and it took hours to recharge the car. Production of the EV1 stopped in 1999 after only around 1,000 cars had been produced.

◄ General Motors installed public charging stations for the EV1. These stations could fully charge a first-generation EV1 in about three hours.

The last fully intact EV1 was donated to the National Museum of American History. However, the EV1 was still very important in laying the groundwork for the first successful electric cars in the 2000s.

A lot of modern car companies began to shift their focus to manufacturing electric cars. The automotive industry began to prepare for a transition to electric engines. In 2022, California announced a plan to ban the sale of all new gas-powered cars by 2035.

By the mid-2020s, most modern cars still used internal combustion engines that ran on gasoline. Gas continued to be a powerful, cheap, and portable energy source. However, cars that run on gas or diesel release greenhouse gases while driving. This contributes to global **climate change**.

An average gasoline-powered car releases several tons of carbon dioxide into the air each year. And every year, tens of millions of new cars are made. All that carbon dioxide adds up in the atmosphere. This makes the atmosphere trap more of the sun's heat, which makes climate change worse. Electric cars will help people drastically cut down on their carbon emissions.

AVERAGE RANGE OF ELECTRIC CARS

An electric car's range is the distance it can drive before it needs to be recharged. One reason that electric cars have different ranges is because they use different kinds of batteries and engines. But a car's range can also change depending on how it is driven.

1999 EV1

70–90 miles (110–145 km) per charge

2019 Chevrolet Bolt

240 miles (390 km) per charge

2022 Tesla Model S

405 miles (650 km) per charge

CHAPTER SIX

SELF-DRIVING CARS

Sarah plays with her car keys and yawns. She's too tired to safely drive herself anywhere. She wishes her car could drive itself. Sarah imagines what that would look like. Wouldn't it be amazing if she could call her car with an app on her phone? Sarah imagines a car pulling into the driveway without a driver behind the wheel. Then, the car would drive itself to her destination. Sarah hopes this will happen in the future.

For centuries, people have dreamed of self-driving machines. Leonardo da Vinci imagined a spring-powered cart that could move by itself along a set path. Francis Houdina operated the first radio-controlled car in 1925.

Many inventions helped pave the way for self-driving cars. One of these was cruise control. Cruise control was first installed by the Wilson-Pilcher company in the early 1900s.

◄ **Summoning a car through the driver's phone might seem like technology of the future, but in the 2020s some car companies were working on similar features.**

▲ **Tesla has started to add self-driving features to its cars. Car technology still has a long way to go before cars can drive without any human control.**

Drivers could pull a lever to make the car continue moving at a set speed. Newer versions can slow the car down if it gets too close to another car.

However, a fully self-driving car goes beyond those features. It is a vehicle that does not need human control at all. A self-driving car can safely respond to any traffic situation and carry people to their destinations.

Self-driving technology could change how people use cars. Instead of leaving cars in garages, people could share them with others. A car could show up only when people need it.

Sharing cars would mean they would be cheaper for everyone to use. Self-driving cars could be safer and more efficient, too. Computers do not get distracted and cause accidents like people do.

Car technology has come a long way since the earliest cars. New inventions have made cars safer and easier to use. Engineers work hard to make cars that are better for the environment. Their research will continue to improve car technology.

THINK ABOUT IT

- Some people want self-driving cars because they'll help eliminate accidents caused by human error. However, some people are worried about the transportation jobs that would be eliminated by self-driving cars. Do you think self-driving cars are a positive development? Why or why not?
- Many car safety features have become standard technology in modern cars. Which car feature do you think is the most important to driver and passenger safety? Why?
- Electric cars have been in production since the 1990s, but they did not become common until the 2010s. Why do you think it has taken so long for them to catch on?

GLOSSARY

climate change (KLY-mit CHAYNJ): Climate change is the long-term shift in Earth's temperature and weather. Greenhouse gases from driving make climate change worse.

combustion (kuhm-BUS-chun): Combustion is the process of burning something. Internal combustion engines burn fuel such as coal or gasoline.

efficient (ee-FISH-ent): Being efficient means completing tasks in an organized and productive way. Lenoir's motor used less fuel than a steam engine, so it was more efficient.

ignition (ig-NISH-uhn): The process of making something burn or catch fire is called ignition. Sparks from an ignition system can start an engine.

patent (PAT-ent): A patent is a form of legal ownership over a specific idea or invention that bans others from using or creating it. Lenoir sold his engine patent because he did not have plans to build the engine himself.

pistons (PIST-unz): Pistons are cylinders that fit inside tubes and move up and down against the liquid or gas inside. Pistons and gears use energy from explosions in the tubes to move machines.

prototype (PROH-tuh-type): A prototype is the first sample of a product that is made to see whether an invention works. Kettering made a prototype of Coleman's self-starter and learned that the invention worked.

torque (TORK): Torque is a measure of the force that causes an object to twist or rotate. The torque in a car's electric motor is powerful enough to start its engine.

SELECTED BIBLIOGRAPHY

"A Brief History of the Internal Combustion Engine." *Tüv Nord*, 18 Apr. 2019, tuev-nord.de. Accessed 2 Nov. 2022.

"Nils Bohlin, 82, Inventor of a Better Seat Belt." *New York Times*, 26 Sept. 2002, nytimes.com. Accessed 2 Nov. 2022.

Spencer, Roy. "40 Years of ABS: Debuted in the S-Class in 1978." *Mercedes Heritage*, 22 Aug. 2018, mercedesheritage.com. Accessed 2 Nov. 2022.

FIND OUT MORE

BOOKS

Kingston, Seth. *The History of Lamborghinis.* New York, NY: PowerKids Press, 2019.

Petersen, Christine. *Inventing the Hybrid Car.* Parker, CO: The Child's World, 2016.

Zettwoch, Dan. *Cars: Engines That Move You.* New York, NY: First Second, 2019.

WEBSITES

Visit our website for links about car technology:
childsworld.com/links

Note to Parents, Caregivers, Teachers, and Librarians: We routinely verify our Web links to make sure they are safe and active sites. So encourage your readers to check them out!

INDEX